Thank you to all my friends who helped,
especially Beth, Barbara, Jasmin, Henri,
Haydn, David, and Susan

Home
Copyright © 2004 by Jeannie Baker
All rights reserved.
Manufactured in China.
For information address HarperCollins
Children's Books, a division of
HarperCollins Publishers,
195 Broadway, New York, NY 10007.
www.harperchildrens.com

The artwork was prepared as collage
constructions, which were reproduced
in full color from photographs taken
by Andrew Payne, Fotographix.
The text type is Simoncini
Garamond.

Library of Congress Cataloging-in-
Publication Data
Baker, Jeannie.
Home / by Jeannie Baker.
  p. cm.
"Greenwillow Books."

Summary: A wordless picture book
that observes the changes in a
neighborhood from before a girl is
born until she is an adult, as it first
decays and then is renewed by the
efforts of the residents.

ISBN 0-06-623935-4
[1. Neighborhood—Fiction. 2. Urban
renewal—Fiction. 3. City and town
life—Fiction.] I. Title.
PZ7.B1742Hl 2004 [E]—dc22
2003049287

First Edition
20 SCP 25 24 23 22

Greenwillow Books

2 YEARS

22 MONTHS

20 MONTHS

18 MONTHS